Ordinary Baby
Extraordinary Gift

Written by
Gloria Gaither

Illustrated by
Barbara Hranilovich

Zonderkidz
The Children's Group of Zondervan Publishing House

In the beginning, God and people were best friends. They were glad to see each other whenever they got together, and when they went for walks in the beautiful garden God had made, they laughed and told each other secrets. They shared everything, and no one was embarrassed or shy.

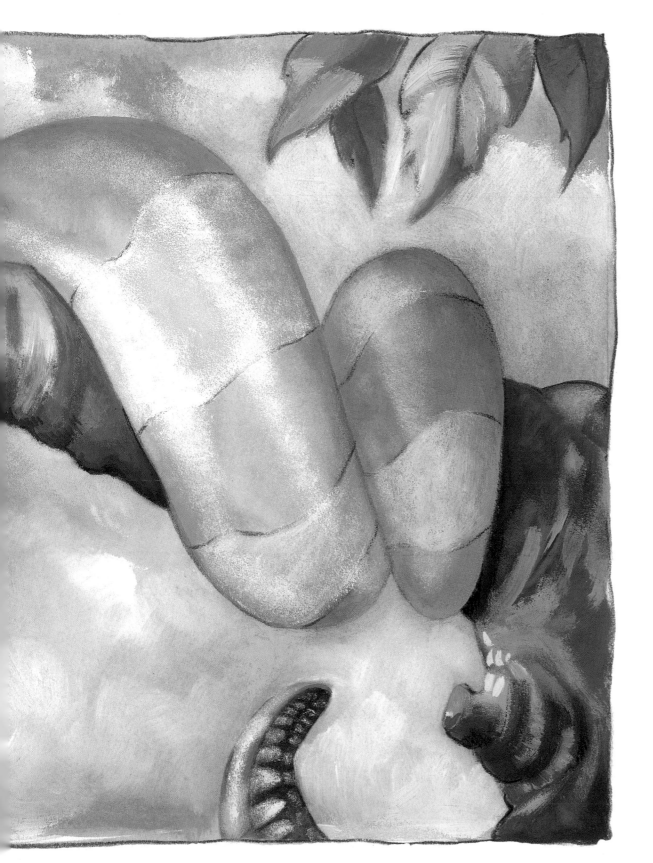

One day, a stranger showed up in the garden—a jealous and selfish creature—and he disguised himself as a beautiful, colorful serpent. He coaxed the two people to break their promises to God and to ruin the wonderful friendship between the people and God.

fterward, whenever God came to enjoy his friends, the people were ashamed and acted guilty and afraid. It was as if God and his friends had become strangers and had no one to introduce them to each other again. God knew everything had changed between them and could never be fixed unless a miracle happened.

From then on, God tried to get messages to his friends about how sad he was to lose them and how very much he loved them. He wrote "I miss you" on the sunset. (That had been the time they took walks.) He pulled at people with gentle breezes that felt like the way the wind blew when they ran together down the garden paths. He hoped the people would remember how close they had been to him.

ver the years, more and more people were born. The mothers and fathers, grandmothers and grandfathers, passed on stories to the children about how God had been best friends with the first man and woman long ago—how they talked and sang and laughed together. The stories seemed almost too good to be true. God was so great, so powerful . . . and so far away. But some of the people who told stories were special listeners. They said they could hear God trying to talk to people. They said he wanted his friends back and that one day he would find a way to fix the friendship the lying snake had destroyed.

The people guessed at how God might do this. Some thought if they could be good enough, God might be friends with them again. They tried so hard to be perfect and to keep all the rules they thought would make God happy. But being perfect was way too hard. The people always went to bed at night disappointed in themselves and sad because they knew this was no way to get to know God again.

The listeners said God would send someone to introduce people to him again, so that God's people could get together with him in a place they called "God's kingdom."

The people talked about what kind of person God would send. The special listeners said God would send a descendent (a child or grandchild or great-grandchild) of a king. That would make him a king too. What kind of king would God send? Certainly, they thought, he'd be a more awesome king than Saul or Solomon or even good King David. He'd be more powerful than the leader of an army. He'd be more rich and fine than the family who lived in the best house in town.

For centuries people waited . . . and wondered. They came up with all kinds of ideas. Some got so tired of waiting they decided the whole story about God was just something someone made up. But it wasn't!

One night in a tiny, tiny town, God kept his promise. And he didn't send someone to introduce people to God—he came himself! And he didn't come as a king riding on a white horse or as a rich man dressed in fancy clothes. He didn't come as a president or a governor. He didn't even come as a grown-up!

No, God had planned all along to come in a way we could understand. He chose to come as a baby, because no one would be afraid of a baby! He knew children might be shy if he came as a grown-up, but no one can be shy around a baby.

Now children could grow up, not in his shadow, but beside him. Like the first people in the garden, children and God would know each other . . . and not be afraid!

So, it was true. God came himself! He was just an ordinary baby born in a simple barn to a loving mother named Mary and a strong man named Joseph, who made things out of wood. Instead of important-looking doctors to help this baby be born, there was just Joseph. Instead of a story in the newspaper, a real star in the sky stopped over the barn and twinkled in the clear dark night.

$\mathcal{W}$ho would have ever guessed it! God thought of the best way to have his friends back. He would be an ordinary baby. That's the way he planned it, maybe, so that we would come to him and not be afraid.

He was just an ordinary baby. That's the way he planned it, maybe
Anything but common would have kept him apart
from the children that he came to rescue,
Limited to some elite few,
When he was the only child who asked to be born.

And he came to us with eyes wide open,
Knowing how we're hurt and broken,
Choosing to partake of all our joy and pain

He was just an ordinary baby;
That's the way he planned it, maybe,
So that we would come to him
and not be afraid.

He was ordinary with exception
Of miraculous conception;
Both his birth and death he planned from the start.

But between his entrance and his exit
Was a life that has affected
Everyone who's walked the earth to this very day.